NORFOLK COUNTY LIBRARY
WITHDRAWN FOR SALE

FOE/CH

D0549275

SAM and JUMP

Jennifer K. Mann

WALKER BOOKS

AND SUBSIDIARIES

LONDON • BOSTON • SYDNEY • AUCKLAND

This is Sam — and Jump.

They do everything together.

Because they are best friends.

One day, they went to the beach ...

where they met Thomas.

Sam and Thomas played all day.

And, when it was time for Sam to leave,
they promised to play again tomorrow.

Sam fell asleep in the car, but when they were
almost home, he awoke with a jolt: Jump!

But it was too dark to go back.

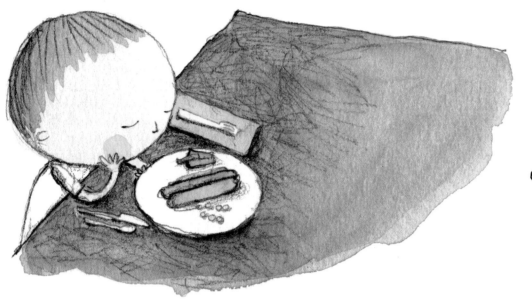

Sam could not
eat his dinner.

Even a bedtime
story didn't help.

"Don't worry," said Mama.
"We'll look for Jump
in the morning."

But Sam couldn't help thinking about all the things that might have happened to Jump.

Early the next morning,
Mama drove Sam to the beach.

But Jump was nowhere to be seen.

Nothing was fun without Jump.

Then Thomas arrived.

Now Sam and Thomas — and
Jump — are best friends.

This one is for my sister, who took me back to the
beach to look for my lost doll. And for my dad, who
made it possible to be at the beach in the first place.

First published 2016 by Walker Books Ltd
87 Vauxhall Walk, London SE11 5HJ

This edition published 2017

2 4 6 8 10 9 7 5 3 1

© 2016 Jennifer K. Mann

The right of Jennifer K. Mann to be identified as
author/illustrator of this work has been asserted by her
in accordance with the Copyright, Designs and Patents Act 1988

This book has been typeset in Providence Sans

Printed in China

MIX
Paper from
responsible sources
FSC® C008047
FSC
www.fsc.org

All rights reserved. No part of this book may be reproduced, transmitted or stored in an information retrieval
system in any form or by any means, graphic, electronic or mechanical, including photocopying,
taping and recording, without prior written permission from the publisher.

British Library Cataloguing in Publication Data:
a catalogue record for this book is available from the British Library

ISBN 978-1-4063-7323-3

www.walker.co.uk